TM & copyright © by Dr. Seuss Enterprises, L.P. 1997
All rights reserved. Published in the United States by
Random House Children's Books, a division of Random House LLC,
a Penguin Random House Company, New York.
Originally published in a slightly different form
by Random House Children's Books, in 1997.
Random House and the colophon are
registered trademarks of Random House LLC.
Visit us on the Web!
Seussville.com
randomhousekids.com
ISBN: 978-0-553-52057-6
Educators and librarians, for a variety of teaching tools, visit us at RHTeachersLibrarians.com
Library of Congress Catalog Card Number: 97-068651
Printed in the United States of America   10 9 8 7 6
Random House Children's Books supports the First Amendment and celebrates the right to read.

Oh, Baby, the Places You'll Go!

adapted by Tish Rabe from the works of

Dr. Seuss

Random House  New York

Dear Reader,

My late husband, Theodor Geisel—
known to most of you as "Dr. Seuss"—
was intrigued by research into the
development of babies while they are in
their mother's womb. The fact that they
could hear sounds—and might actually
respond to the voices of their parents—
was both exciting and mystifying to him.

Some years ago, Ted and I came
across an article about some researchers
who had asked prospective mothers and
fathers to read aloud to their babies in
utero. To our delight, the book they read
was *The Cat in the Hat.* The researchers
found increased uterine activity during
the reading, and a gradual settling
down afterward. This response to the
book continued after delivery. The baby
apparently recalled having heard the story
before . . . *in utero!*

Ted loved his involvement in this bit of prenatal research.

This book is joyfully dedicated to Ted and to all you parents in the process of getting to know that most significant other (or others) . . . in utero.

Audrey Geisel
La Jolla, California

WELCOME!

Baby, oh, baby,
the places you'll go!
The worlds you will visit!
The friends you will know!

The horn-tooting apes
from the Jungles of Jorn
will hoot a big toot
on the day you are born.

While a bird flying high
from far off in Katroo
will sing on the wing,
"Happy Birthday to *you*!"

(Then the Once-ler will call
on his Whisper-ma-Phone
with a secret he's saving
for your ears alone.)

You will find from your very
first moment in space
you're surrounded by new friends
all over the place!

There's Daisy-Head Mayzie
and Cindy-Lou *Who,*
Hunches in bunches
and Lolla-Lee-Lou.

The Curious Crandalls,
the Brothers Ba-zoo,
the Star-Belly Sneetches—
the Wump of Gump, too.

Bartholomew Cubbins,
Marco, and Max,
and also the North-
and the South-Going Zax.

There's Thidwick, who lives
with his friends in a bunch
at a lake where there's lots
of sweet moose-moss to munch.

A very tall cat
in a red-and-white hat
who loves to do tricks
in West Gee-Hossa-Flat.

A boy with his yo-yo
(the youngest McCave)
and his 22 brothers,
who all are named Dave.

And a worm who can see
all the way to Japan,
which is quite a bit farther
than anyone can.

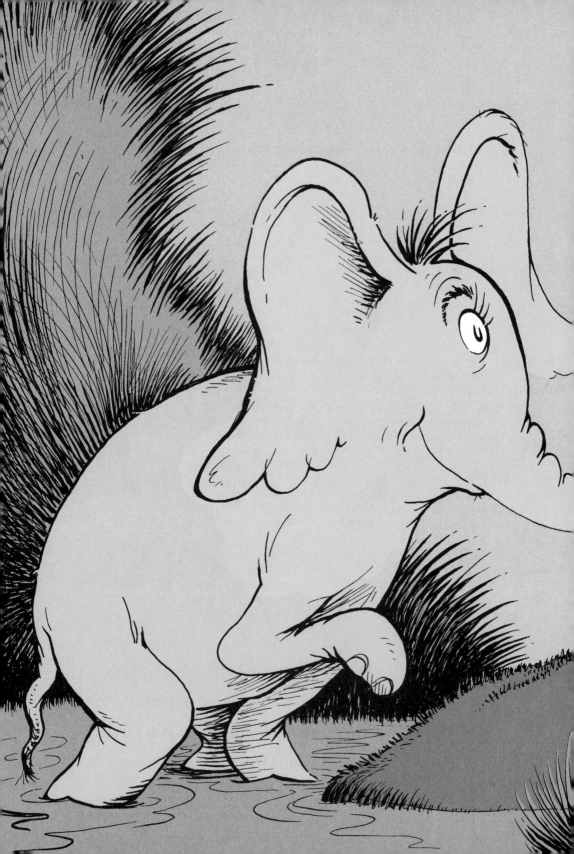

And Horton, who lives
in the Jungle of Nool,
every fifteenth of May
in the cool of the pool,
will show you the dust speck
that houses the *Whos,*
those brave little folks
we would not want to lose.
He saved their whole town,
for he knows, after all,
a person's a person,
no matter how small.

Soon you will meet
a young man, Sam-I-Am,
and get your first taste
of his green eggs and ham.

And speaking of eggs, try some
Scrambled Eggs Super
Special Deluxe
à la Peter T. Hooper!

You're also invited
to have some roast beast—
every Christmas in *Who*-ville,
it's really a feast.

You will visit great places
no speller can spell,
like the country of
Motta-fa-Potta-fa-Pell,
where you'll ride on a
Fizza-ma-Wizza-ma-Dill.
(You'd better do it, 'cause no one else will!)

Then take a quick trip
out to Sala-ma-Sond,
where Yertle the Turtle
was king of the pond,
till a turtle named Mack
did a plain little thing:
he burped . . .
and he toppled
the throne
of a king!

You will sit by the edge
of McElligot's Pool—
where the fish, just like you,
spend their days in a school.

And you'll find that it's fun
when you hop on your pop,
but don't be surprised
when he asks you to STOP!

On beyond Zebra,
you'll find a new letter,
like Yekk, Yuzz, or Wum,
that will make your life better.

And *you'll* have a story
that no one can beat
when you say that you saw it
on Mulberry Street.

But whatever you do,
things won't *always* go right.
You might meet the Grinch
in the dark of the night.
His heart is too small
and his shoes are too tight.
(He's not very friendly
and rarely polite.)

You may run into trouble,
as folks often do,
when you're trying to travel
to Solla Sollew—
like that world-famous
Zanzibar Buck-Buck McFate,
who got caught in the traffic
on Zayt Highway Eight . . .

While you are growing,
we're all busy counting
the days till we meet you—
excitement is mounting!

We've saved you a seat
at the first matinee
of the Circus McGurkus
(there are four every day),
where Great Daredevil Sneelock,
the world's bravest type,
will be pulled through the air
by three Soobrian Snipe
on a dingus contraption
attached to his pipe!

Here are two tickets
(for you and a guest)
to the new zoo, McGrew Zoo—
it's really the best.
It's there you will see
the great Russian Palooski.
This zoo, it is true,
has not one-ski, but two-ski.
Their headskis are redski;
their bellies are blueski.
(I'd try not to miss them, if I were you-ski!)

You'll find that this world's
a great place to begin,
but it *could* use some help—
which is where *you* come in.

So now, as my voice
burble-urps in your ear—
with a bump-thumpy sound
that is not very clear—
the words I am saying
you hear in your heart,
and know that I wish you
the very best start.

It's a scrumptulous world
and it's ready to greet you.
And as for myself . . .

well . . .
I can't wait to meet you!

STORYBOOKS WRITTEN AND ILLUSTRATED BY DR. SEUSS